THIS WALKER BOOK BELONGS TO:

_____

_____

_____

_____

First published 1988 by
Walker Books Ltd
87 Vauxhall Walk
London SE11 5HJ

This edition published 1989

8 10 9

Text © 1988 Sarah Hayes
Illustrations © 1988 Jan Ormerod

Printed in Spain

British Library Cataloguing in Publication Data
A catalogue record for this book is
available from the British Library.

ISBN 0-7445-1328-6

EAT UP,
GEMMA

Written by
Sarah Hayes

Illustrated by
Jan Ormerod

WALKER BOOKS
AND SUBSIDIARIES
LONDON • BOSTON • SYDNEY

One morning we woke up late.
I couldn't find my shoes
and Gemma wouldn't eat her breakfast.
"Eat up, Gemma," said Mum,
but Gemma threw her breakfast on the floor.

Later on we went to the market.
Mum bought a bag of apples
and some bananas.
The man at the fruit stall
gave me a bunch of grapes.
He gave some to Gemma too.
"Eat up, Gemma," said the man,
but Gemma pulled the
grapes off one by one
and squashed them.

When we got home
Grandma had made the dinner.
"Nice and spicy," Dad said,
"just how I like it."
It was nice and spicy all right.
I drank three glasses of water.
"Eat up, Gemma," said Grandma.
Gemma banged her spoon on the table
and shouted.
But she didn't eat a thing.

The next day was Saturday
and Dad took us to the park.
We had chocolate biscuits for a treat.
I ate two and then another two.
"Eat up, Gemma," said Dad.
But Gemma didn't eat her biscuit.
She just licked off all the chocolate
and gave the rest to the birds.

In the evening our friends
were having a party.
"Eat up, everyone," said our friends.
And we did, all except Gemma.
She sat on Grandma's knee
and gave her dinner to the dog
when Grandma wasn't looking.

After the party my friend came to stay
and we had a midnight feast.
Gemma didn't have any.
She was too tired.

In the morning we made Gemma a feast.
"Eat up, Gemma," said my friend.
Gemma picked up her toy hammer
and banged her feast to pieces.
My friend thought it was funny,
but Mum and Dad didn't.

Soon it was time for us to put on
our best clothes and go to church.
I sang very loudly.

The lady in front of us
had a hat with fruit on it.
I could see Gemma looking and looking.

When everyone was really quiet
Gemma leaned forward.
"Eat up, Gemma," she said.

Then she tried to pull
a grape off the lady's hat.
She pulled and pulled
and the lady's hat fell off.
Gemma hid her face in Dad's coat.

When we got home I had an idea.
I found a plate and a bowl.
I turned the bowl upside down
and put it on the plate.
Then I took a bunch of grapes
and two bananas and put them on the plate.
It looked just like the lady's hat.

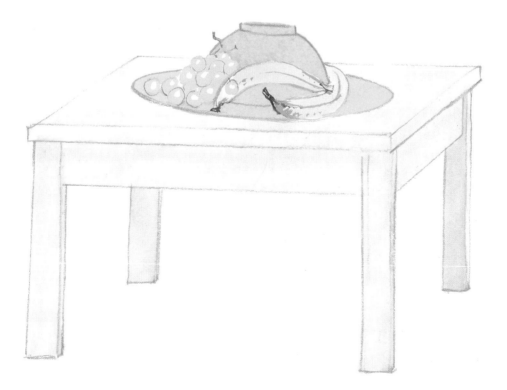

"Eat up, Gemma," I said.
And she did.
She ate all the grapes
and the bananas.
She even tried to
eat the skins.

"Thank goodness for that," said Mum.
"We were getting worried," said Dad.
Grandma smiled at me.
I felt very proud.
"Gemma eat up," said Gemma,
and we all laughed.

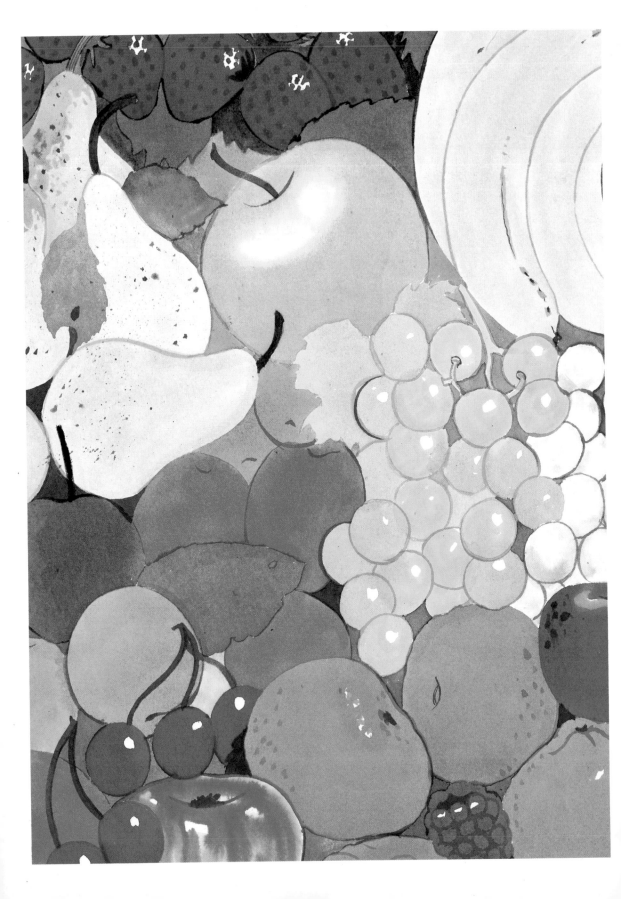

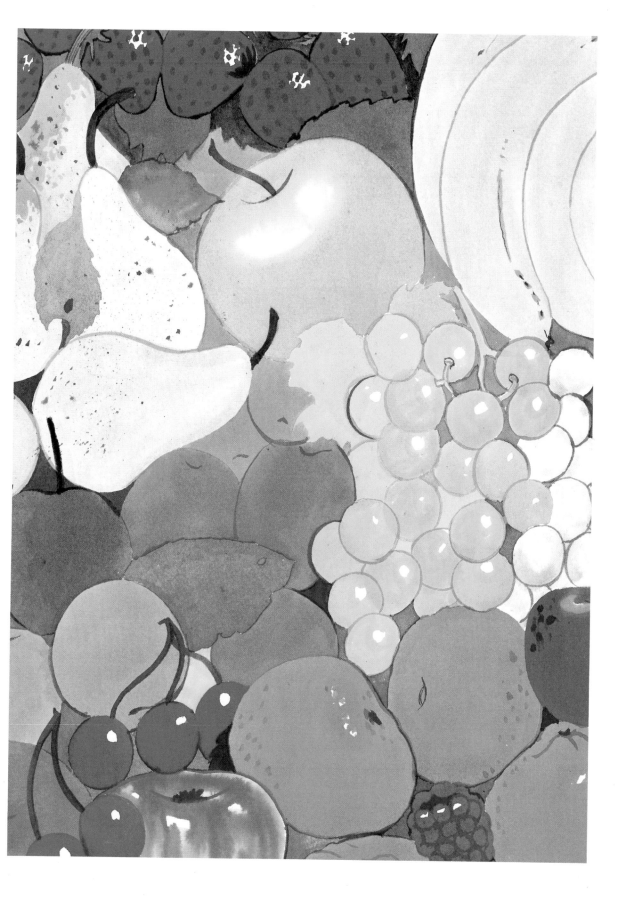

MORE WALKER PAPERBACKS
For You to Enjoy

Also by Jan Ormerod

HAPPY CHRISTMAS, GEMMA
written by Sarah Hayes

Shortlisted for the Smarties Book Prize and
Highly Commended for the Kate Greenaway Medal.

"One of my favourites… All children, no matter what their colour,
will be able to see themselves in this delightful Christmas story."

Floella Benjamin, The Daily Mirror

0-7445-1022-8   £3.99

MIDNIGHT PILLOW FIGHT
A small girl wakes in the middle of the night
and discovers her pillow wants to play!

"Jan Ormerod is a master of this genre – her ability
to catch the playful whimsical mood … an idea perfectly matched
by the artist's creativity and exquisite skill." *Books for Keeps*

0-7445-3642-1   £3.99

THE FROG PRINCE
"Beautifully retold with illustrations that are stunningly effective."
Practical Parenting

0-7445-1787-7   £3.99

WHEN WE WENT TO THE ZOO
"Wonderful animal pictures … the book as a whole adds up
to a great experience for a child." *Tony Bradman, Parents*

0-7445-2318-4   £4.99

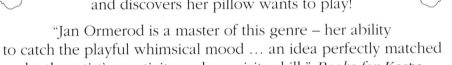

Walker Paperbacks are available from most booksellers, or by post from B.B.C.S., P.O. Box 941, Hull, North Humberside HU1 3YQ
24 hour telephone credit card line 01482 224626

To order, send: Title, author, ISBN number and price for each book ordered, your full name and address,
cheque or postal order payable to BBCS for the total amount and allow the following for postage and packing:
UK and BFPO: £1.00 for the first book, and 50p for each additional book to a maximum of £3.50.
Overseas and Eire: £2.00 for the first book, £1.00 for the second and 50p for each additional book.
Prices and availability are subject to change without notice.